Word Wise with Wordsworth

a breath of fresh air—a welcome change (**idiom, page 26**)

beyond—on the far side of something (**preposition, page 7**)

careen—to move in a fast and out-of-control way (**verb, page 15**)

cluster—a close, small group (**noun, page 14**)

confusion—a panicked or disorderly situation (**noun, page 21**)

considerate—when you think about other people's needs and feelings (**adjective, page 25**)

eager—very interested to do something (**adjective, page 29**)

expression—a phrase or saying that has a particular meaning (**noun, page 11**)

gawk—to stare in an obvious way (**verb, page 19**)

gurgle—to make a low, bubbling sound (**verb, page 12,** *gurgled*)

impressive—very good in a way that gets someone's attention (**adjective, page 24**)

lively—up-beat and energetic (**adjective, page 10**)

murmurs—quiet expressions of a feeling (**noun, page 23**)

peeved—to feel annoyed or irritated (**adjective, page 9**)

qualified—to have the skills required to do a particular task (**adjective, page 17**)

reasoning—figuring out something in an orderly way (**noun, page 12**)

situation—something that is going on at a certain time (**noun, page 23**)

speculate—to make guesses or think carefully about something (**verb, page 8**)

structure—something that has been built (**noun, page 20**)

trudge—to walk slowly with a lot of effort (**verb, page 26,** *trudged*)

wonder—to think about something yo̶ ̶ ̶ ̶k̶n̶o̶w̶ ̶m̶o̶r̶e̶ ̶a̶b̶o̶u̶t̶ (**verb, page 18**)

A BREATH OF FRESH AIR

by Quinn Alexander
Illustrated by Kelly Kennedy

SCHOLASTIC INC.

New York Toronto London Auckland Sydney
Mexico City New Delhi Hong Kong Buenos Aires

When the doors of Nathan T. Webster Elementary School opened, Marco and Abby were the first in line to enter the building and the first to enter their classroom. Their teacher, Mrs. Harris, was busy writing on the board. So Marco went straight to his desk and took out the mysterious map that he and Abby had discovered the day before. Meanwhile, Abby raced over to the large bird cage by the windows. Wordsworth, the class's pet bird, was sitting on a perch with his eyes half closed.

"Hi, Wordsworth. How are you doing?" asked Abby. "You look sleepy." She lowered her voice to a whisper. "Did our big adventure wear you out? Are you tired from going back and forth in time?" Abby continued. "You can tell me. It's just me and Marco here—and Mrs. Harris, but she's not paying attention."

Wordsworth ignored her.

"Come on, say something!" Abby begged. "I know you can talk."

Wordsworth opened his eyes wide. "Find your seat. Find your seat," he said, raising his crest feathers.

"I don't mean copy-the-teacher talk," said Abby. "I mean *real* talk. Whole sentences, like the kind you used yesterday," Abby said.

But Wordsworth wasn't looking at her. He was looking **beyond** her at the students entering the classroom.

Abby sighed. She went over to Marco's desk and studied the map he had spread out. "Anything new?" she asked.

"Nope," Marco said. "I was hoping some more buildings would show up besides the schoolhouse. But nothing did. The map still has lots of empty spaces." He tucked it back in his desk. "I'll check it again later on."

As it turned out, Mrs. Harris kept the class busy with lessons that day, and Marco and Abby had no time to **speculate** about talking cockatoos and strange maps. But the minute school was over, it was a different story. While Mrs. Harris graded papers at her desk, both Abby and Marco moved to the table by Wordsworth's cage and opened the books they had borrowed from the library. They were staying late again so that they could work on their project about the history of Cloverhill. But they were also hoping to figure out how to travel back in time, as they had the day before.

After a while, Mrs. Harris stood up and stretched. "I need a break," she said. "I'm going to the teachers' room for some coffee. I'll be back in a moment. Keep up the good work, kids."

"Keep up the good work," echoed Wordsworth, as Mrs. Harris left the room.

"Yeah, yeah. We heard what Mrs. Harris said," Abby muttered. She still felt a little **peeved** with Wordsworth for ignoring her earlier.

The bird began hopping around his cage. "Pay attention, pay attention," he called over and over. It was more copy-the-teacher talk. But then he added something new, "Open the door! Open the door!"

"That's it! That's what he said yesterday," said Marco. "He must have been waiting for Mrs. Harris to leave."

He and Abby opened the cage door and Wordsworth flew straight out of the room and into the hallway, with the two of them running after him.

Mr. Keys, the custodian, was in the hallway, mopping the floor and singing a **lively** tune. He broke off as Wordsworth flew around his head. "Loose *again*?" Mr. Keys said to the bird. "That's okay. I suspect you'll end up in the same place as yesterday."

Sure enough, Wordsworth zipped into Mr. Keys's room and headed for the supply shelves at the back. Marco and Abby followed him. This time, they weren't quite so surprised when the shelves vanished into the darkness and the walls became a tunnel. But they still weren't prepared for the loud pop and the flash of bright light. They blinked and looked around in a daze and found that they were inside a building with a wood floor, tall windows, and a high ceiling. Wordsworth was nearby, sitting on the arm of a wooden bench.

"Startling, isn't it?" the bird said. "I'm not sure I'll ever get used to the feeling."

"You mean you've done this before?" asked Marco. "Before yesterday, I mean?"

"Oh yes—on many occasions," said Wordsworth. "I'm sure you've heard the **expression** 'time flies.'"

"Well yes," said Marco. "But doesn't that just mean that time passes really fast?"

Abby was getting impatient. "Never mind that," she said. "I figured out where we are—the Cloverhill train station. The building still looks the same as in our time. But we're wearing the same kind of old-fashioned clothes we had on the last time, so it must be a hundred years ago."

"Excellent **reasoning**," Wordsworth said, bobbing his head.

"Why are we *here*?" asked Marco. "Last time, we helped save the school. But the train station doesn't need saving." He looked at Wordsworth. "Wait, I know what you're going to say: 'You kids are smart. You'll figure it out.'"

"Exactly," said Wordsworth.

"Well, there's nothing going on in here," Abby pointed out. "Let's try outside."

Wordsworth hopped onto her shoulder, and they all left the station and walked into bright sunshine. It was a beautiful day. Birds called to one another, trees rustled in the breeze, and the nearby Big Muddy River splashed and **gurgled**. But gradually, these gentle sounds were drowned out by the huffing and puffing of a train heading toward the station.

"It's a steam engine!" Marco yelled over the noise. "I had a toy train just like it."

There was a loud screech of brakes and the train came to a stop.

With a squawk, Wordsworth flew into the air.

"Wordsworth! Come back!" Abby called.

But the bird disappeared over the trees, heading toward a
cluster of buildings down a street.

"We had better go after him," said Marco. "I'm sure he wouldn't
leave us alone here in the past. But I would feel a whole lot better if I
knew where he went."

The two of them took off. They were in such a hurry that they
ran right into a tall woman who was stepping down from the train.
The bag she was carrying went flying and it spilled onto the platform.

"Oh, my gosh! I'm so sorry. We were kind of in a hurry," said Abby. "We were chasing—"

"A *friend*," Marco added quickly, "and we didn't see you."

"I guessed as much," the woman said with a smile. "You probably don't **careen** into strangers on purpose. And there's no damage done—at least not to me. But I'll have to gather my belongings."

"We'll help you," Abby offered. "I'm Abby, by the way, and he's my friend Marco."

"I'm Sara Thompson," said the woman.

As the train pulled out of the station, the three of them gathered up the woman's things. Among them, Marco found a stethoscope. "Are you a doctor?" he asked, returning it to the bag.

The woman narrowed her eyes. "Yes, I am. I'm *Doctor* Thompson," she said. "Does that surprise you? I can assure you that I graduated from the Women's Medical College of Pennsylvania, and I am fully **qualified**. Perhaps you've never met a female physician before. There aren't many of us, at least not yet."

"In our time . . . I mean, *town*," Abby said, quickly correcting herself, "our family doctor is a woman, too."

"Really?" said Dr. Thompson. "I'd love to meet her and compare medical stories."

Abby and Marco looked at each other in alarm, but fortunately, Dr. Thompson didn't seem to notice their concern.

"Too bad that won't be possible," Dr. Thompson went on. "I'm just changing trains here—on my way to Chicago to interview for a job at a hospital." She smiled at the kids. "Well, it was very nice to meet you. But I'm afraid I've made you miss your friend."

"Wordsworth!" Abby gasped. "I forgot all about him."

"That's our friend. *Mister* Wordsworth," said Marco. He quickly grabbed Abby's arm. "Come on, Abby. Let's go find him. Good-bye, Dr. Thompson."

"Good-bye. I hope you find your friend." said Dr. Thompson. She turned and entered the train station.

Marco and Abby set off down the platform.

"Wordsworth was heading for those buildings," Abby said, pointing. "Let's check over there first."

"OK," said Marco. "I think that's downtown Cloverhill. I mean, it's where downtown would be a hundred years from now, because this is the way we would walk to downtown from *our* train station, which is really the same as *this* train station, only—"

"Marco, stop!" cried Abby. "What we really have to do is find Wordsworth *now*."

"Right," said Marco. "But this time-travel stuff is really cool. It made me **wonder**—are we in two places at once? Do we have two different bodies?"

Abby just sighed without answering.

Soon they were walking down the main street of town. People in old-fashioned outfits were entering and leaving various shops, and a couple of horse-drawn carriages passed. It was hard for the kids not to **gawk**. It was like seeing history come alive.

"Okay, this is definitely Washington Avenue," Abby said. "That's the bank my parents use. But the bookstore is missing and the toy store is, too. I guess they came later. Or maybe—she stopped short and turned to Marco. "Maybe that's why we're here—to make sure the new places get built."

Suddenly Abby and Marco saw a flash of something white on a two-story building ahead.

"Wordsworth!" shouted the kids.

They hurried to the next cross street, but there was no sign of the bird. Instead, they saw a building that was under construction. Wooden scaffolding was set up and a crew of five men was plastering a wall.

"Maybe that's what we saw—the white plaster, not Wordsworth," said Marco.

As he and Abby watched, some of the upper boards suddenly gave way. One man fell onto the lower boards, then another. Then the whole **structure** started to sway and pull away from the building. Some of the workers managed to jump clear of the falling masonry, but two others were not so lucky. They became trapped under the scaffolding as it broke apart and crashed to the ground.

There was a moment of terrible silence, then a lot of shouting and **confusion** as everyone came running to help.

"Who has a cell phone? Call 911—call 911!" Abby yelled. Then she remembered where she was and clapped her hand over her mouth.

One of the workers took charge. "You, you, and you," he said, pointing to three strong-looking men. "Help us clear away the scaffolding. Everyone else, stay back."

"Is there anything we can do to help?" Marco asked a man in a suit and black hat. "Is there an ambulance that can take people to the hospital? Should we run and get a doctor?"

The man looked at Marco curiously. "I guess you aren't from Cloverhill," he said. "The closest hospital's in Franklin, five miles away; and we haven't had a doctor in town since old Doc Sanders retired and moved away two months ago."

"But there *is* another doctor in town—at the train station," said Abby. "Come on, Marco. Let's go get her."

"'Her'?" said the man.

But Abby and Marco were already running toward the station.

In a matter of minutes, they reached the station and explained the **situation** to Dr. Thompson. Concerned, she grabbed her medical bag and quickly followed them. When they reached the site, the injured men had been freed from the broken scaffolding.

"This is Dr. Thompson," Abby said loudly. "She's come to help."

The townspeople looked at Dr. Thompson in surprise. There were **murmurs** from the crowd. "A woman? A woman doctor?"

But she ignored them and went straight to the injured men. It was quickly clear that she knew what she was doing. She sent one person off to get clean cloth for bandages. She sent others for soap and water, along with blankets to serve as stretchers to carry the men inside. She even used the workers' plaster to make casts for one man's broken leg and another's broken arm.

When Dr. Thompson was finished and the injured men had been taken home, the other workers and the townspeople gathered around and thanked her.

"Very **impressive**," said the man in the suit. "You stayed calm, and you got the job done."

"And you've got a good hand with plaster," added one of the thankful workers.

Dr. Thompson smiled. "I'm glad I could help," she said. "It seems I was in the right place at the right time."

Abby nudged Marco. "We were, too," she whispered.

"I understand you were at the station," said the man in the suit. "May I ask where you were headed?"

"Chicago. I'm interested in taking a job at a hospital there," said Dr. Thompson.

"I'm afraid you've missed the train," said the man. "There isn't another one till tomorrow."

"May I offer you a room for the night?" said one woman. "I'm Mrs. Russo. My husband and I own the inn, on Adams Avenue."

"Why, thank you," Dr. Thompson said. "That's very **considerate** of you."

The man in the suit tipped his hat. "I'm Mr. Bennett. I run the bank," he said. "As long as you're stuck here, perhaps we could show you around. Cloverhill's a nice town. You might like the place, and we sure could use a doctor."

Dr. Thompson smiled. "Even a woman doctor?"

"Why not?" said Mrs. Russo. "You'd be **a breath of fresh air** after old Doc Sanders. He was pretty set in his ways by the time he retired."

"Well, you're looking for a job. And we need a new doctor," said Mr. Bennett. "At least think about it over tonight."

"All right," Dr. Thompson promised. "I'll think about it."

Some of the townspeople started to walk away. "We should go, too," Marco said to Abby.

"Yeah, but I want to know if Dr. Thompson stays in Cloverhill," said Abby.

"Maybe the map will show us when we get home," suggested Marco. "Anyway, I think we did what we were supposed to do. We still have to find Wordsworth—and the way home."

"OK," said Abby. "Let's return to the train station. That's where we started out."

They **trudged** back to the station. They spotted Wordsworth, sitting on a cart.

"Hello," he said, hopping onto Marco's shoulder. "I see you're ready to go home. So open the door."

Abby opened the station door. Nothing happened.

"Maybe it's a door *inside* the station," said Marco. They tried several other doors, but all of them were locked. Then they tried one that led to the ticket booth and opened it. It was dark inside.

"This *has* to be it," said Abby.

She grabbed Marco's hand, and they stepped inside. Once again, there was a loud pop and a flash of light, and they were back in Mr. Keys's room in the school building. A moment later they stumbled into the hallway.

Mr. Keys was still mopping the floor. "That was quick," he said. "Back to your cage, Wordsworth."

The kids were **eager** to check the old map, so they didn't stop to chat with the custodian. They raced back to the classroom and put Wordsworth in his cage. But they barely had time to retrieve the map and sit down before Mrs. Harris returned with her coffee.

"I'm back," she said, heading for her desk.

Abby grinned at Marco. "So are we," she whispered.

Marco unfolded the map. A small brick building had appeared on one of the side streets. The door had a sign that read Dr. Sara Thompson.

"Good work," said Wordsworth.

Get Your Word's Worth

After you finish reading this book together, use the prompts below to spark thoughtful conversation and lively interaction with your child.

♣ Abby was **eager** to go on another adventure with Wordsworth and Marco. What are you eager to do? Why?

♣ The crowd thought Dr. Thompson was **impressive** because she knew how to care for the hurt workers. Name two people or things that have gotten your attention today. Why?

♣ **Trudge** is much more elaborate than walking. Trudge to the kitchen and back.

♣ Marco was hoping the map would be filled in when they returned to school, but it wasn't. If you had to **speculate** about the map, why are there still empty spaces?